The Count of Monte Cristo

Adapted by
Rob Lloyd Jones

Illustrated by Victor Tavares

Reading consultant: Alison Kelly
Roehampton University

Contents

The sails of the *Pharon* shimmered in the winter sun as the ship came into Marseilles docks. Edmond Dantes climbed onto the bowsprit, gazing wide-eyed across the clutter of warehouses that lined the waterfront. It had been a long and difficult voyage, and he was thrilled to be home.

But on the docks, Mr. Morrel, the ship's owner, greeted him with a worried frown. "Where is Captain Leclere?" he asked.

Edmond smiled sadly. He told Mr. Morrel how Captain Leclere had died of fever. As second mate, he had taken command of the ship himself for the rest of their trade voyage.

"But there is something Dantes has not reported," a voice said.

It was Danglars, the ship's accountant. He was a shrewd-looking man who always had a sneer on his face, especially for Edmond.

"Edmond has not said that we stopped at Elba," he told Mr. Morrel.

Morrel's face darkened. The island of Elba was where France's previous ruler, Napoleon Bonaparte, was being held prisoner. All ships were banned from stopping there.

"Is this true?" Mr. Morrel asked.

"It is," Edmond said. "Before Captain Leclere died, he asked me to deliver a letter to the island."

"Then it is settled," Morrel announced. "Edmond was simply loyal to his captain. As I am sure others will be to him."

"You mean *Edmond* is to be made captain?" Danglars seethed.

"I do," Morrel said. "If you accept Edmond?"

A beaming smile spread across Edmond's face. Him – a captain! But before he could reply, he saw a beautiful young woman running towards him through the crowds. It was Mercedes, his fiancée.

Mercedes leaped into Edmond's arms, blushing with delight. As they kissed, though, Edmond spotted a gloomy figure watching them from the shadows.

"Who are you sir?" he demanded.

Mercedes pulled the man closer. "Edmond, this is my cousin Fernand. He looked after me while you were away."

Edmond grasped Fernand's hand and shook it firmly. "Then you can be the first to hear the news Fernand. I am to become captain of the *Pharon*, and tomorrow Mercedes will become my wife!"

Laughing, Edmond twirled Mercedes in his arms. He was so happy right then. So happy, in fact, that he failed to notice the jealous hatred in Fernand's eyes...

Chapter 2

Conspiracy

Waves crashed angrily against the jetty as Fernand Mondego stormed to the end of the dock. His whole body trembled with rage. He couldn't bear to see Mercedes with another man.

"Why did Dantes ever return?" he cried.

"Be careful what you say," a voice answered. "Edmond has many friends around here."

Danglars sat outside a tavern, with his accounts papers spread across a table.

"What do you want?" Fernand spat.

"Merely to share a toast," Danglars said, pouring a glass of wine. "To Edmond Dantes, future captain of the *Pharon* and husband to the fair Mercedes."

Fernand's face turned livid red. He snatched Danglars' glass and smashed it to the floor. "I hate Edmond Dantes!" he cried.

Calmly, Danglars poured himself another drink. He too hated Dantes. He had worked hard on the *Pharon*, and felt that it should be him, not Edmond, who was made captain.

"What if there was a way to make him go away again?" he said. "You could marry Mercedes and I would become captain."

"If only there was," Fernand groaned, "then I would do it, however hard."

Danglars' lips curled into a sinister smile. He rustled among his papers, finding a blank sheet. Then he dipped his quill into his inkpot.

"It is not hard at all," he said. "We simply have to write a letter."

The following night, at the same tavern
where Fernand and Danglars wrote their
letter, excited guests gathered for Edmond
and Mercedes' wedding feast. Edmond wore
his best suit and his biggest smile, while
Mercedes' eyes sparkled with joy. Everyone
agreed that they had never seen such a
happy couple.

The tavern rang so loudly with laughter
that no one heard the miserable moan from
the back of the room.

Fernand sat with his head hung in despair. "I cannot bear to watch," he told Danglars. "You said that our letter would solve everything. But still Mercedes is about to be married."

"Have faith," Danglars said. "I think I hear our plan working now..."

Just then, five soldiers marched into the tavern, armed with rifles. Their captain stormed up to Edmond. "Edmond Dantes?" he said. "I arrest you in the name of the law."

Mercedes reached to hold Edmond back, but the young sailor simply smiled and stepped forward.

"You must be mistaken," he said. "I have never committed a crime in my life."

The captain waggled a sheet of paper in Edmond's face. "This letter says otherwise."

"Dear sir, it is my duty to inform you that Edmond Dantes, mate of the ship Pharon, recently docked at the island of Elba carrying a letter for the traitor Napoleon Bonaparte."

"Who wrote this?" Edmond asked.

"Do you deny that it is true?"

"I do not, but –"

"Then you must come with us."

Before Edmond could reply, the soldiers grabbed his arm and yanked him away. As they dragged him from the room, he saw the startled faces on all of his guests – except for two. Fernand and Danglars were smiling.

Dark clouds gathered over the docks as the soldiers marched Edmond from the tavern. One of the men thrust him into a boat and the others climbed in beside him. They began rowing from the dock.

"Please," Edmond begged, "where are you taking me?"

"See for yourself," one of the men grunted.

And then Edmond did. They were headed for a craggy island beyond the bay, from which a stone fortress rose to the soot-black sky. That fortress was Chateau D'If, a grim prison for traitors.

Suddenly, Edmond flung himself across the boat. But before he could escape over the side, one of the guards clubbed him on the head with his rifle.

Edmond slumped to the watery deck. He lay groaning, too dazed to fight, as the boat bashed against another dock. The guards lifted him from the deck and up some stone steps.

Lightning blazed across the sky. Chateau D'If loomed over Edmond in ghastly silhouette. Thunder roared around the old prison's crumbling walls.

Edmond was hurled into a dingy cell. One of the guards leaned over him, his face ghostly white in the glare of his lantern. "Welcome to your new home," he said.

The door slammed shut. Edmond was left alone in the dark.

Chapter 4

The two prisoners

For hours, Edmond sat slumped against the cell wall, clutching his knees to his chest. He was convinced he would be released any moment. But that moment never came.

Hours turned into days. Slowly, Edmond's confusion boiled into anger. Each time the guards brought him food, he smashed the bowl against the door and yelled until his voice ran dry. "I am innocent!" he cried.

Days became weeks and then months. Edmond curled up in the dark, haunted by memories. At first he thought about Mercedes, but more and more he became obsessed with Fernand and Danglars. He was certain they wrote the letter accusing him of treason.

Months grew into years. By then, Edmond's wedding suit hung like rags around his skeleton frame. His nails grew long and filthy, and lice crawled in his tangled beard.

All day the scurrying sound of rats echoed around his cramped cell. The noise seemed to be coming from under the ground. Edmond pressed his ear to the floor, listening for hours. How he envied their freedom!

Then, one day, the ground began to tremble. One of the stones shuddered and rose.

Edmond scrabbled back in fright as a head emerged from the ground – a tangled mass of white hair and beard with two bulging eyes in between. It was another prisoner!

The old man glared at Edmond cowering in the corner. "Curses!" he cried. "I have dug the wrong way. I thought I was escaping the prison, not digging deeper inside."

Edmond crawled closer and peered into the man's tunnel. For the first time in years, a smile spread across his filthy face. "Let me help you dig in the other direction," he said.

"It would take years," the man replied.

"I have years."

The old man smiled, showing his black and brown teeth. "So do I," he said. "Follow me!"

Edmond slid into the tunnel and wriggled like a worm through the narrow space. He rose into another cell, as dark and dingy as his own.

The old man bowed. "My name is Abbé Faria," he said.

"Abbé?" Edmond replied. That meant priest. "Why are you in prison?"

"Because I knew a secret that I wouldn't tell the King."

"What secret?"

The old man smiled again.

"It is a secret," he said.

The Abbé skipped across his cell and tapped one of the stones in the opposite wall. "If we dig this way for about five years, we should come out near the sea."

He handed Edmond a digging tool made from a bent iron bed leg. "Let's get started."

That first night, they barely dug an inch into the wall. But each night after, Edmond crawled from his cell and they continued scraping at the rock.

As they dug, Edmond told the Abbé about Mercedes, and his hunger for revenge against Fernand and Danglars. But whenever he asked about the Abbé's secret, the priest just smiled and kept digging.

Each night they met, and each night the tunnel grew longer. Then, around twenty years after Edmond was thrown into Chateau D'If, the Abbé called excitedly from the end of the tunnel. "Edmond, I see daylight!"

Edmond's heart raced. They had reached the end. But as he scurried closer, the tunnel walls began to tremble. Zigzag cracks splintered along the roof.

"Abbé!" Edmond cried. "Come back."

But it was too late. Rocks crashed down as the tunnel collapsed.

Chapter 5

Escape from Chateau D'If

Heavy rocks rained down on Edmond as he struggled back through the collapsing tunnel. He managed to grab hold of the Abbé's legs and drag the old priest back to his cell. The Abbé's eyes rolled. He was badly hurt.

"I'll call the guards," Edmond said.

But the Abbé held him back. "No," he said weakly. "Listen to me..."

The Abbé pointed a shaky finger at a stone on the wall. "Look behind that stone."

Confused, Edmond dug his fingers around the edges of the rock. It was loose. He pulled it away, and found a scrap of paper behind. "It's a map," he said.

"Of the island of Monte Cristo," the Abbé explained. "It shows where treasure is buried. This, Edmond, is my secret. And now that I die, the treasure is yours."

The Abbé slumped to the floor.

He was dead.

Tears stung Edmond's eyes. Was he now doomed to die alone in this place? He heard footsteps and dived back into the tunnel to his cell. He lay in the dark, listening to the guards discover the priest's body.

"Old fool," one of them said. "Looks like he died trying to escape. What shall we do with the body?"

"Wrap it up," another replied. "We'll get rid of it tonight."

The guards left. Cautiously, Edmond rose from the tunnel. The Abbé's body lay covered in a sack on the floor. Suddenly Edmond knew how he could escape.

Moving fast, he pulled the sack from the Abbé and dragged the body down into the tunnel. Then he rushed back and wrapped the sack around himself instead. He had the Abbé's map in his pocket, along with his digging knife. He'd let the guards bury him outside the prison, and then dig himself free.

After several hours, the guards returned. Edmond's heart hammered so hard he was sure it would give him away, as the guards picked him up and carried him from the cell.

"He's heavy for an old man," one of the men muttered.

Edmond heard a door creak open. For the first time in twenty years, he breathed fresh air. He was outside. Through a hole in the sack, he glimpsed the edge of the cliffs. Where were the guards going to bury him?

One of the men grabbed Edmond's leg and lashed a rope around his ankles. To Edmond's horror, he saw a cannonball attached to the other end. He realized now what was happening. The guards weren't going to bury him at all.

They picked him up... and flung him off the cliff!

Chapter 6
The fisherman's replies

Edmond plunged
into the icy water.
He wriggled free of the
sack, but he was dragged
deeper by the cannonball
attached to his legs. He felt
as if his lungs were on fire.
Then he remembered
– the knife! He grabbed
the blade from his pocket
and cut the rope, freeing
himself of the weight.

He burst to the surface,
but now a wave slammed
him against a fishing boat
tethered to the rocks.
Exhausted, Edmond just
managed to cling onto the
side of the boat and haul
himself up onto the deck.

But there was no time to rest. Soon the guards would discover Edmond had escaped. With his last gasps of strength, he rowed and rowed until Chateau D'If was just a shadowy speck in the distance.

Ahead, he could see lights glimmering on Marseilles' docks. Edmond had dreamed of his home for twenty years, but the sight gave him no joy. All he thought of was revenge.

Another fishing boat passed. Edmond called to the captain. "I am headed to Marseilles to surprise an old friend. Do you know a man named Danglars?"

"I did once," the fisherman replied. 'But he moved to Paris. I hear he is a rich banker now, called Baron Danglars."

"What about Fernand Mondego?"

"He too is a rich man. He lives in Paris with his wife and son Albert."

Edmond couldn't believe it. While he had been rotting in jail, his enemies had grown rich. "Do you know a girl named Mercedes?" he asked.

"You are truly out of luck," the fisherman laughed. "She lives in Paris too. She is Fernand's wife."

Edmond slumped to the deck. More than ever, he craved revenge. A plan was forming in his head. First he would go to Monte Cristo and find the Abbé's treasure. Then he would disguise himself as a rich noble like his enemies. He would enter their lives. And he would destroy them.

Almost one year after Edmond's escape from prison, a carriage clattered up to the most magnificent hotel in Rome. Two young men stepped out. One was Beauchamp, a writer from Paris. The other was Albert Mondego, the son of Mercedes and Fernand.

"This is the finest hotel in Rome!" Albert declared. "Surely it is the perfect place to watch the carnival."

But inside, Albert's smile disappeared.

"I'm afraid all of our rooms have been taken," the hotel manager said. "By one man."

"What sort of man would take over an entire hotel?" asked Beauchamp.

Albert was already marching upstairs to find out. He had boasted to his friends that he'd be staying in this hotel, and would look like a fool if he was not. But before he could decide which door to knock on, one of them flew open. A servant bowed.

"Gentlemen," he said, "the Count of Monte Cristo is expecting you."

"Expecting us?" Albert said. "What a peculiar thing."

Inside, the room was decorated like a palace, with tapestries on the walls and magnificent paintings in golden frames. Albert had never seen such luxury.

"My father knows all of Europe's noblemen," he told Beauchamp, "but I've never heard of the Count of Monte Cristo. Who is this man?"

A door flew open and in swept Edmond Dantes. His face was disguised by a neat beard and he wore a velvet cloak, intricately

embroidered with gold. He introduced himself as the Count of Monte Cristo.

"Gentlemen," the Count said, bowing gracefully, "I hoped you would join me to watch the carnival from my balcony."

As the Count led the way, Albert whispered to Beauchamp. "How mysterious! His skin is as white as snow. It is as if he has been living underground."

Fireworks fizzed into the sky as the carnival began. Costumed performers paraded through the streets, dancing, juggling and singing songs. As Albert and Beauchamp watched, the Count charmed them with tales of his travels around the world.

"But it is Paris that I would most like to visit," he said.

"My dear Count," Albert said. "I live in Paris! You *must* come and visit."

"I would love to," said the Count. "Can you recommend a banker in the city to look after my money?"

"There is none finer than Baron Danglars," Albert replied. "And you can meet my father too, Fernand Mondego."

A muscle twitched in the Count's neck. "Perfect," he said. "I will come in exactly one month, at three o'clock."

As more fireworks exploded over the balcony, Albert leaned to Beauchamp. "What a magnificent man!" he whispered. "I cannot wait for him to meet my parents."

Chapter 8

Paris

Exactly one month later, at precisely three o'clock, the doorbell rang at Albert's home in Paris. The Count of Monte Cristo entered, dressed immaculately in the finest French fashion and a velvet cloak.

"My dear Count," Albert said. "I had begun to think our meeting in Rome was a dream."

"If only all dreams were as pleasant," the Count replied.

Albert led the Count into the drawing room, where two men rose and bowed.

"This is my father," Albert said, "Fernand Mondego. And this is Baron Danglars, the richest banker in all of Paris."

The Count's pale face flushed red as he came face to face with the men who ruined his life. They didn't recognize him, but he knew them immediately. Danglars had the same pompous sneer on his face, while Fernand remained a gloomy figure, despite the golden military medals on his coat.

"Those are fine medals," the Count said.

Fernand puffed out his chest. "I won them defending a fortress against Turks in Greece."

"My father made his fortune while in Greece," Albert added eagerly.

"And what happened to the fortress?" asked the Count.

"I am afraid that it was lost."

Danglars poured the Count a glass of champagne. The baron glanced greedily at the Count's emerald rings. "Albert tells me that you require the services of a banker," he said. "My customers have accounts with me of over a million francs."

"A million francs?" said the Count, laughing. "Why ever would I need a bank for such a trifling sum? I have two million in my pocket right now."

Danglars was lost for words. The Count spoke so simply he was either telling the truth or he was mad. But before he could ask which, a door opened and a woman entered dressed in a flowing silk gown.

It was Mercedes. She saw the Count and froze. Her mouth cracked open and a tiny gasp came out.

"Are you ill Mother?" Albert asked. "You look suddenly pale."

The Count simply bowed. "It is a look that suits you well madame," he said. "And now that I have met you, I am afraid I must leave. I only came to invite you all to a party at my new house in Paris."

The Count smiled and left. But inside his carriage, he sat back and groaned. Had Mercedes recognized him? It was strange seeing her after so long. But he felt no love, only hatred for Fernand and Danglars. He thought he might have killed them right then. But death was too good for them. He planned to make them suffer...

Chapter 9

The Count's party

For the next few weeks, there was only one name that interested anyone in Paris society – the Count of Monte Cristo. At plays, operas and dinners, everyone asked about this mysterious man and his magnificent wealth.

As if to answer, the Count threw a lavish party at his new house. All the richest nobles arrived dressed in their most stylish clothes and dripping with jewels. But everyone's eyes were on the Count, as he moved gracefully among his guests.

None of the guests studied their host closer than Mercedes. As the Count passed, she took his arm. "It is hot in here, Count," she said. "Perhaps you would take a walk with me in the garden?"

For a second, the Count's calm smile vanished and panic flashed across his face. Mercedes took his arm and they strolled among elegant fountains and lime trees hung with twinkling Chinese lanterns.

"Albert tells me that you have sailed all over the world Count," Mercedes said. "I wonder if you ever met a sailor named Edmond Dantes?"

The Count flinched. "I have not madame. Is he a friend?"

"He was a man I loved. But I was told that he died in prison, many years ago."

The Count flinched again. His jaw clenched. "Who told you that?" he demanded.

But before Mercedes could reply, Danglars interrupted their walk. "Excuse me Count," he asked, "but I wonder if you have given any thought to my services as a banker?"

The Count turned. He looked at Danglars with awful calmness. "Very well Baron," he said, "the time has come. Follow me."

The Count led Danglars into his drawing room, where he opened a wooden chest. "I would like you to look after my entire fortune," he said.

Danglars' eyes glinted with greed. The chest was filled with diamonds, rubies and emeralds that glimmered like a rainbow in the gaslight.

"Can you take them to your bank immediately?" asked the Count.

Without another word, Danglars picked up the chest and carried it from the room.

The Count smiled grimly. His plan for revenge had begun. "Your greed ruined my life Danglars," he said to himself. "Now watch as it ruins your own."

Chapter 10

The Roman catacombs

It wasn't the weight of the Count's treasure that made Danglars' arms tremble. It was excitement. He had hoped to become the Count's banker, but now he had a new idea. He would steal the Count's fortune! "Take me to Rome!" he called to his driver.

The carriage rode for hours. Danglars dozed and dreamed about how he would spend the Count's treasure. At last they came to a sign pointing to Rome. But the carriage turned in the other direction.

"Driver," Danglars called, "we are going the wrong way."

But the carriage didn't turn. Danglars glimpsed a hooded figure in the driver's seat – a bandit? Had he been kidnapped?

The carriage finally stopped and the door creaked open. The hooded man aimed a pistol at Danglars. "Get out," he said.

Danglars climbed from the carriage, clutching the Count's treasure. They had reached the Roman catacombs, underground tombs cut deep into the rock. The hooded man pushed Danglars through a dank passage and into a cramped cell. A door slammed shut behind him.

Danglars sat in dismal darkness. He didn't understand why the bandit hadn't taken the treasure. After several hours, he banged on the door. "At least bring me some food!" he cried.

The door creaked open. The hooded man placed a plate of succulent roast chicken on the floor. Danglars reached for it greedily, but the hooded man raised his pistol.

"This meal costs ten diamonds," he said.

Danglars hesitated. Ten diamonds was a ridiculous price, but he had no food and plenty of treasure. He threw the man the jewels and pounced on the plate. "But you'll get no more jewels from me!" he warned.

Danglars was wrong. He resisted for as long as he could, but eventually his hunger got the better of him. He paid ten emeralds for roast beef, and then fifty rubies just for water.

After several days, there were only three diamonds left in the Count's chest. Those jewels were all Danglars had left. Two days passed and he didn't eat. He grew weak and desperately hungry. He sank to his knees, clutching his aching stomach. "Why do you make me suffer?" he pleaded.

The door opened. The hooded man stepped inside the cell. "Suffer?" he said. "There are men who have suffered worse."

"No," Danglars groaned, "there are none."

"I will show you one," the hooded man replied. Slowly, he peeled back his hood and revealed his face.

"The Count of Monte Cristo!" Danglars cried.

The Count grabbed Danglars' collar. His eyes were red and wild with rage. "No!" he seethed. "I am the man whose life you ruined twenty years ago. I am Edmond Dantes!"

Danglars fell back in horror. He curled up sobbing and shaking.

"Now your life is ruined too," said the Count, as he took the last jewels from his chest and strode from the cell. "Fernand," he whispered, "you are next..."

Chapter 11

Challenge at the opera

Two days later in Paris, Albert Mondego stormed into the office of his friend Beauchamp. He waved a newspaper at the journalist. "Have you read this?"

Beauchamp's face darkened as he read the report. The newspaper called Albert's father a traitor. It claimed to have evidence proving that, years ago, Fernand surrendered a Greek fortress to enemy Turks for money. *That* was how Fernand made his fortune.

"Where is your father now?" Beauchamp asked Albert.

"Soldiers are searching for him all over Paris," Albert said. "You have friends at this paper, Beauchamp. Find out what evidence they have."

Soon after, Beauchamp returned. He had a worried frown on his face. "The newspaper received a document," he told Albert. "It is the contract agreeing the surrender of the fortress to the Turks. Albert, it's signed by your father."

"It is a fraud!" Albert insisted. "Some unknown enemy is acting against my father."

"Not unknown," Beauchamp said. "My friend at the newspaper knew exactly who gave him the document. Albert, it was the Count of Monte Cristo!"

The pair raced to the Paris Opera House,

where Albert knew the Count would be that evening. He pushed through the crowds and stormed down the aisle, to where the Count sat sipping champagne.

"I demand an explanation," Albert said.

"An explanation?" the Count replied. "At the opera? Surely this is not the place, my friend."

"You are no friend of mine, Count. Are you an enemy of my father?"

A gasp echoed around the stalls. Everyone watched as the Count rose. His glare was so fierce that Albert stepped back in fright.

"I am," the Count said.

"I demand to know why," Albert replied.

"I cannot tell you."

"Then I challenge you to a duel. We will meet tomorrow morning with pistols. Good day sir!" With that, Albert turned and strode away.

The Count straightened his coat and returned to his seat, as if he wasn't remotely bothered by Albert's attack. But he was. He *had* given the document to the newspaper, but in the hope that Fernand would challenge him to a duel, not Albert.

Perhaps, though, this was a better revenge. He planned to kill Fernand. But if Fernand wouldn't fight, he would kill his son instead.

On stage, the curtain rose and the final act began.

Chapter 12

Duel in the park

BOOM!

The blast from the Count's pistol echoed around the park, scattering pigeons from the trees. The shot hit the trunk dead in the middle. The Count's aim was perfect.

The Count rubbed his tired eyes. He hadn't slept at all last night. He had come here to punish Fernand by killing his son. But he felt a sadness… Was he doing the right thing?

A carriage approached, and Albert stepped out with Beauchamp. His eyes were red and puffy and his pistol trembled in his hand. He had clearly not slept either.

"Count," he said, "tell me what cause you have to hate my father."

"I cannot."

"Then we must fight."

Beauchamp stood between the two men. "Gentlemen," he instructed, "you must each take ten paces and then turn and fire."

The duel began.

The Count raised his pistol and began pacing. *One…two…* He thought about his life before Chateau D'If, and the man he once was. Happy Edmond Dantes…

Four…five… He thought of Fernand, and how he had stolen that happiness.

Seven… eight… The Count's finger curled around the trigger.

Nine… ten! The Count turned.

"EDMOND!"

The Count froze. Mercedes raced across the park. Tears streamed down her cheeks. "Edmond!" she gasped. "Please spare my son!"

But the Count's pistol remained fixed on Albert. "Edmond is dead," he said coldly. "I am simply an angel of vengeance."

"But why Edmond? Why do you seek revenge? Fernand has done nothing to you."

The Count's whole body trembled with rage. "Nothing?" he cried. "Because of him, I rotted in jail for twenty years."

"No," Mercedes said, "not Fernand…"

"You do not believe me? Here is the proof!"

The Count pulled a crumpled paper from his pocket and threw it to Mercedes. It was the same letter that, twenty years ago, accused him of treason. Only then, the soldiers had hidden the signatures at the bottom. One of them said Danglars. The other belonged to…

"Fernand Mondego," Mercedes whispered. Her legs buckled and she fell weeping to the long grass.

Albert read the letter too. His pistol slipped from his hand. But still the Count kept his weapon aimed at Albert's head. His hand shook. He gazed at Mercedes, crying at his feet. Slowly, he lowered the pistol.

"Edmond," Mercedes sobbed.

"No," the Count said softly. "I do not know who I am anymore…"

Chapter 13
Wait and hope

Fernand Mondego jumped breathlessly over the fence and into the back garden of his house. He hid in the shadows, making sure he hadn't been seen. His darkest secrets were now public, and he was hunted by the army. If he was caught, he would surely hang.

He crept into his house and hurriedly filled a case with clothes. He planned to flee to Marseilles and then hide on a boat to Africa.

Just then, he heard footsteps. Fernand watched through a crack in the door as Mercedes and Albert came down the stairs. They too carried bags. And they were with the Count of Monte Cristo.

"Come Mother," Albert said, "this is no longer our home."

The words stabbed like a knife in Fernand's heart. He had lost everything! But then he heard something even worse. As Mercedes left, she turned to the Count and said, "Thank you Edmond."

Fernand sunk to the floor. The Count of Monte Cristo was Edmond Dantes!

There was a loud knock on the back door. Soldiers gathered in the garden. They had seen Fernand inside, but Fernand was too stunned to move. Even as they smashed down the door, he just curled on the floor, muttering the name of the man who had ruined him…"Edmond…
Edmond Dantes…"

The Count walked Mercedes and Albert to their carriage. He heard the commotion inside the house, but he didn't care. His obsession with revenge had already gone too far, almost killing poor Albert. It was over. He never wanted to hear the name Fernand Mondego again.

Neither did Mercedes or Albert. They were moving to Italy, far from the scandal that had shamed their family.

"You could come with us," Mercedes said, as the Count helped her into the carriage.

But the Count just smiled. He took her hand and kissed it gently.

"I cannot," he said. "I have lived all this time for revenge. Now, I must live for something new. I will find a new life."

As the carriage rattled away, Mercedes leaned from the window. "Edmond, how do you know that you will find this new life?"

The Count closed his eyes, feeling the warm winter sun soothe his pale skin. "I will wait," he said. "Wait and hope."

Alexandre Dumas

1802-1870

Alexandre Dumas was born in France in 1802. His father was a General in the army, and died when Alexandre was only four. He lived quietly with his mother in the country until he was 21, when he went to Paris to seek his fortune. Dumas became famous as a writer of plays and books, including *The Count of Monte Cristo* and *The Three Musketeers*. He was one of the first authors to write lively, exciting, historical stories and combine them with romance and adventure.

Designed by Michelle Lawrence
Digital manipulation: Nick Wakeford
Series designer: Russell Punter
Series editor: Lesley Sims

First published in 2010 by Usborne Publishing Ltd., Usborne House, 83-85 Saffron Hill, London EC1N 8RT, England. www.usborne.com
Copyright © 2010 Usborne Publishing Ltd.